Horace and Morris but mostly Dolores

To my daughter, Zoey, and in memory of her grandmother,
Lonnelle Crossley Howe
—J. H.

To my mom and dad, with thanks to Judy Sue
—A. W.

ISBN 0-439-11475-6

Text copyright © 1999 by James Howe. Illustrations copyright © 1999 by Amy Walrod.
All rights reserved. Published by Scholastic Inc., 555 Broadway, New York, NY 10012,
by arrangement with Atheneum Books for Young Readers, Simon & Schuster Children's
Publishing Division. SCHOLASTIC and associated logos are trademarks
and/or registered trademarks of Scholastic Inc.

12 11 10 9 8 7 6 5 4 3 2 1   0 1 2 3 4 5/0

Printed in the U.S.A.   14

First Scholastic printing, March 2000

Book design by Ann Bobco and Angela Carlino
The text of this book is set in Gararond-Bold.
The illustrations are rendered in acrylic paint and collage.

Horace and Morris but mostly Dolores

written by JAMES HOWE

illustrated by AMY WALROD

SCHOLASTIC INC.
New York Toronto London Auckland Sydney
Mexico City New Delhi Hong Kong

Horace and Morris but mostly
Dolores loved adventure.

They sailed the seven sewers.

They climbed Mount Ever-Rust.

They dared to go where no mouse had gone before.

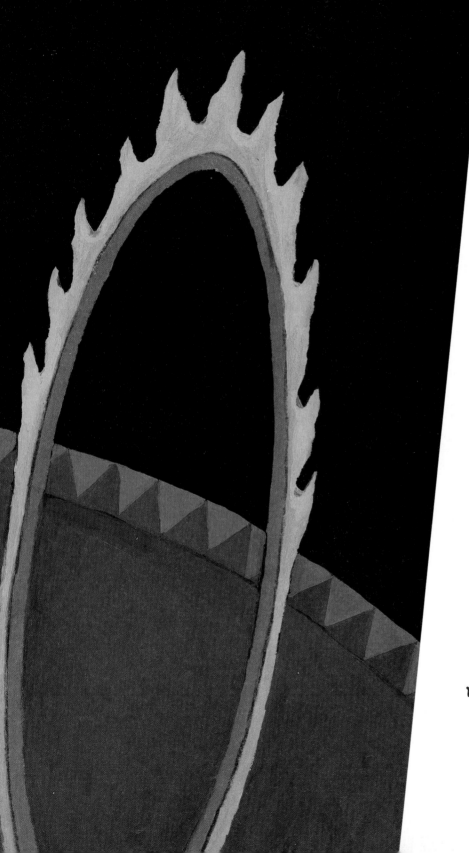

Horace and Morris
but mostly Dolores
never said,

"This is something we shouldn't do."

They said,

"**This is
something
we've
got to do!**"

And so there was almost
nothing they didn't do.

Horace and Morris
and Dolores were friends—
the greatest of friends,
the truest of friends, the
now-and-forever-I'm-yours
sort of friends.

And then one day . . .

Horace and Morris had a decision to make.

They didn't want to do anything without Dolores,
but as Horace pointed out, "A boy mouse must do what a boy
mouse must do."

"Bet you can't say *that* three times real fast," Dolores said
with a smile.

Horace and Morris didn't even try.

They didn't even smile.

"Good-bye, Dolores," they said.

MEGA-MICE
NO
GIRLS
~~ALLOWED~~ ALLOWED

What kind of place doesn't allow girls?
Dolores wondered as she watched her friends step
through the door of the Mega-Mice clubhouse.

Downhearted,
Dolores
went on her way—
alone.
It wasn't long
before . . .

The Cheese Puffs no boys allowed

Dolores had a decision to make.

She didn't really want to do anything without Horace and Morris, but she figured a girl mouse must do what a girl mouse must do.

(She said this aloud three times real fast just to prove that she could.)

A GIRL MOUSE MUST DO WHAT A GIRL MOUSE MUST DO. A GIRL MOUSE MUST DO WHAT A GIRL MOUSE MUST DO. A GIRL MOUSE MUST DO WHAT A GIRL MOUSE MUST DO.

I'll bet Horace and Morris couldn't do that, she thought. But she wasn't smiling as she stepped through the door of the Cheese Puffs clubhouse.

TODAY'S PROJECT:
GIFTS FOR
MOTHER
MADE FROM
Muenster

Day after day, Dolores went to the Cheese Puffs. Day after day, Horace and Morris went to Mega-Mice. They missed playing with each other, but as they said . . .

A GIRL MOUSE MUST DO WHAT A GIRL MOUSE MUST DO.

Horace and Morris and even Dolores were sure their friendship
would never be the same. But then one day . . .

Dolores made a different decision.

"I'm bored," she announced.

The other girls stared.

"Anybody here want to build a fort? How about a Roque-fort?"

The other girls booed.

"Okay, forget the cheese. I'm sick of making things out of cheese anyway. Let's go exploring."

The other girls gasped.

"Phooey!" said Dolores. "I quit!"

"If you quit, then I quit, too!" a small voice said from the back of the room.

Outside, Dolores introduced herself. "I'm Dolores."

"I'm Chloris," said the girl. "Now where can we go to have some *real* fun around here?"

Dolores thought and thought. "I've got it!" she said at last.

The five friends spent the rest of the day exploring.
Chloris and Boris and Horace and Morris . . .

but mostly Dolores....

And the next day they built a clubhouse of their own.